Hunter, Mollie,
1922-

The Knight of the
Golden Plain

$11.70

DATE			

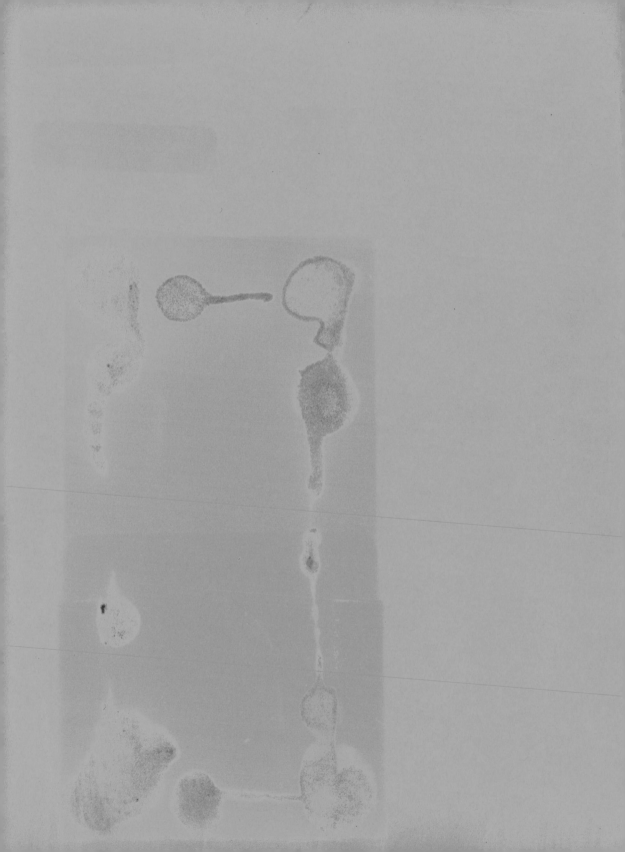

The Knight
of the
Golden Plain

A CHARLOTTE ZOLOTOW BOOK

The Knight of the Golden Plain

by Mollie Hunter

illustrations by
Marc Simont

Harper & Row, Publishers

The Knight of the Golden Plain
Text copyright © 1983 by Maureen Mollie Hunter McIlwraith
Illustrations copyright © 1983 by Marc Simont
Printed in the U.S.A. All rights reserved.

Library of Congress Cataloging in Publication Data
Hunter, Mollie, date
  The Knight of the Golden Plain.

  "A Charlotte Zolotow book."
  Summary: In a young boy's daydream, he becomes a
strong and fearless knight and rides off to do good
deeds and find great adventure.
  [1. Imagination—Fiction.   2. Knights and knighthood—
Fiction] I. Simont, Marc, ill. II. Title.
PZ7.H9176Kn 1983   [E]   82-48747
ISBN 0-06-022685-4
ISBN 0-06-022686-2 (lib. bdg.)

First Edition

To my grandsons,
Roderick McIlwraith,
Douglas McIlwraith,
and
Ian McIlwraith,
with much love from
Mollie Hunter

If you were dreaming one day of the adventures you would like to have, who would you choose to be? And what would you do then?

There was a boy once, who decided to be a knight — a strong and fearless knight. And in his dream ...

The Knight of the Golden Plain rode out to do good deeds and to seek great adventures. It was a Saturday, which gave him the entire day for this. Also, it was summer and the sun was shining, which made him all the more eager to be on his way.

The Knight, of course, was very brave; so brave, in fact, that he had won for himself the name of Sir Dauntless. He had a sword by his side. He was mounted on a great black horse called Midnight, and he wore armor of silvery chain mail under his scarlet jerkin.

"Giddyup, Midnight," the Knight ordered, and flicked the horse's reins that were of the same scarlet color as his own jerkin.

The great black horse galloped out into the sunshine. *Thud, thud,* went his hooves. *Thud, thud,* echoed the sound far and wide over the Golden Plain. And immediately then, all the witches and dragons there knew that Sir Dauntless was riding forth.

The witches grew pale with a terror that made them forget how to cast their spells. The dragons crept back into the furthest corners of their dark

caves. The witches also tried to hide. But Sir
Dauntless had keen eyes, and already he had seen
both the dragons and the witches.

For the next half hour or so Sir Dauntless rode
back and forth, hunting down the witches and
banishing them from his domain.

They fled before him, yelling and shrieking. But
Sir Dauntless was not afraid of their wild voices.
They cursed him with evil words far too shocking
to be repeated here. But Sir Dauntless was pure in
heart as well as brave. He closed his ears to the
sound of the evil words, and continued riding back

and forth until he had hunted down all the witches
and banished every last one of them.

The noble Sir Dauntless turned his attention
then, to the dragons.

One by one he found the caves where they hid.
Outside each cave he stood and shouted his challenge; and one by one those huge and fierce
creatures charged forth to do battle with him.

They rose into the air on their wide, leathery wings and swooped down again to attack with their long and cruelly sharp talons. They roared and snorted great bursts of fire and smoke at him.

Sir Dauntless set Midnight wheeling and circling to avoid the fiery dragon breath. He met the swoops from the air with powerful strokes of his sword. And one by one the attacks of the dragons grew weaker.

One by one he dealt them the fatal wound that brought even the biggest of them down before him in a pool of foul green dragon blood; until finally, he had slain them all.

The dragon slaying took Sir Dauntless rather more time than he had needed for hunting down the witches. It had been thirsty work, too, on such a hot day; and by the end of it all he was more than glad to find a stream where he and Midnight could have a drink of cool, clear water.

Sir Dauntless bathed his face in the stream when he had finished drinking. Then he picked some flowers of clover and sucked the honey from them while he tried to think what he should do next.

"I shall ride till I see a castle," he decided at last. "And then, if there is a beautiful maiden in distress there, I will rescue her."

Up again onto Midnight's back went Sir Dauntless.

He was feeling very pleased with the good deeds he had done thus far. With all the witches gone, also, and all the dragons dead, he never even suspected that everything he now did was being watched—and all because of the witches he had banished.

They had fled, those spiteful creatures, straight

to the only one who could give them revenge on Sir Dauntless. They had fled to their master, the mighty demon Arriman; Arriman, who was also the most cunning of all magicians. And it was his dread gaze that was spying now on every action of the bold Sir Dauntless.

Still with no idea that this was so, however, Sir Dauntless put Midnight to the trot.

Ahead of him, the Golden Plain stretched so far that it seemed to have no end, and everywhere on it was the glitter of sunshine. Sir Dauntless whistled cheerfully as he rode on through this bright and peaceful scene; and every now and then—just to keep in practice for dragon slaying—he slashed away with his sword at the heads of dandelion flowers.

In the distance, after a while, he saw a shape that could have been a dark and very big rock. On the other hand, the shape could easily have been that of a castle.

Sir Dauntless stared hard at the shape, squinting his eyes against the sun; and the more he stared and squinted, the more sure he became that he was indeed looking at a castle.

"And if that is so," he told himself, "I had better hurry to see if there is a maiden in distress there."

With his sword held ready to meet any danger that might lie ahead, he urged Midnight to a gallop. And silently behind him, still, came the dark and lurking form of Arriman.

The castle that might have been a rock was called Crag Castle. And as soon as Sir Dauntless decided it was indeed a castle and not a rock, things began to happen there.

A soldier appeared on the battlements and ran a flag up something that had looked like a tall, thin spur of rock, and that now looked like a flagpole.

Some children ran out into the castle courtyard and began throwing a bright-colored ball to one another.

Cooks and other servants grew suddenly busy in the kitchen.

And suddenly also, there was a stir of movement from a tall figure standing at the window of a room high up in a tower of the castle.

The tall figure was the knight Sir Veritas. His face was sad, and he had been standing very still beside the window—as still as the stone of the castle itself.

There were two other people in the tower room with him—his wife, the Lady Honoria, and their daughter, Dorabella. These two others also looked sad. And they also were as still as stone.

The Lady Honoria had some sewing on her lap, but her hand had stopped halfway through making a stitch. Dorabella sat before a mirror with a comb held poised above her hair.

Then came the moment when the soldier with the flag and the children with the ball and the servants in the kitchen all stirred into action; and when Sir Veritas also stirred.

In that same moment, too, Lady Honoria's hand moved to carry her needle through its stitch, and Dorabella brought her comb down through a tress of her long hair.

Sir Veritas turned from the window. With a smile beginning to lift some of the sadness from his face, he told the other two:

"My dears, I have just seen someone riding towards Crag Castle; a knight in scarlet, mounted on a great black horse."

"A knight!" Lady Honoria exclaimed. "Then let us hope he is a brave one, and also that he will be willing to help our daughter."

Dorabella said nothing. Dorabella had blue eyes, eyes of starry sapphire blue. And her long hair was golden, palest moongold. She was beautiful, and she was her parents' beloved only daughter, but still she did not speak. She could not, because her voice had been stolen from her.

Tears gathered, instead, in her eyes; great glittering tears that quite drowned their starry blueness.

Sir Veritas could not bear to see his darling daughter in tears; and quickly he said:

"The knight certainly looks brave, Dorabella. He rides very boldly."

"And if his heart is pure," Lady Honoria added, "his courage will not fail—not even against the evil that has struck us here in Crag Castle."

Dorabella was comforted by all this. And as she went on combing her moongold hair, she wondered if the stranger knight would be not only brave and pure in heart, but handsome also.

S ir Dauntless was given a tremendous wel-
come at Crag Castle.

All the dogs in the castle came running
to greet him, and Sir Veritas ordered a great feast in
his honor. Lady Honoria made sure he was given

large helpings of everything served at the feast—especially when it came to his favorite dessert, which was strawberries and cream.

The dogs that had come running stayed with him to wait for their share of the feast. Big hunting dogs, small household dogs—every kind he could imagine was there, right down to a litter of puppies that were like balls of black and brown and gold fur tumbling around at his feet.

Sir Dauntless ate and ate, till he was afraid he would burst. Then he leaned back in his chair, took one of the puppies on his knee, and sat gazing at Dorabella.

She was, he thought, the most beautiful girl he had ever seen—so beautiful, in fact, that it gave him a pain in his heart to look at her. And the more he felt this pain, the more sure he became that it meant he was falling in love with her.

He could not help noticing, however, that Dorabella looked very sadly back at him. Also, that she had eaten nothing of the splendid feast—not even the strawberries and cream. And why, he wondered, did she never speak?

Sir Veritas guessed what Sir Dauntless was thinking. "My daughter is in great distress," he

said, "because her voice has been stolen from her."

Sir Dauntless was astonished at this. "How could such a thing happen?" he asked.

Sir Veritas sighed, and told him, "It was when Dorabella had her last birthday. The Lady Honoria and I gave a party for her then; and because we wanted the whole world to see how beautiful she is, we invited as many people as possible to the party. But there was one person we did *not* invite— one who is so hateful that we could not bear to have him near our darling Dorabella. And that was the demon magician, Arriman."

Sir Veritas had no sooner spoken the name of Arriman than the demon himself showed his powers.

A blast of foul-smelling air blew suddenly over them all. The flames of the fire in the fireplace turned from red to an eerie, flickering blue. The puppy on the knee of Sir Dauntless began to shiver with fear, and all the other dogs set up a mournful howling.

Sir Dauntless stared around to see if he could find the cause of all this. But Arriman, of course, was too clever to let himself be seen at that moment.

Then Sir Veritas raised his voice over the dogs' howling, and cried:

"But Arriman came to the party, all the same! He came in his demon robes of slime green and rusty black and rotting purple; and he roared in his demon voice that he would be revenged for the way we had offended him.

"Then he thrust his dreadful green face close to the beautiful face of Dorabella, and breathed his hot and stinking breath on her. The instant she felt this, her voice came out of her in the shape of a tiny golden singingbird that flew straight into the hand of Arriman.

"And so long as he holds that bird captive, Dorabella cannot speak."

The noble heart of Sir Dauntless was much moved by so tragic a tale.

"Tell me," he said, "where and how is the singingbird held captive?"

"In the Dark Forest that lies just beyond Rapid River," Sir Veritas answered; "in a little silver cage fixed to a tree at the center of the Forest. But I have not told you the worst of it yet, Sir Dauntless, and the worst is this.

"The little bird sings every time it sees itself in a mirror. And Arriman has lined the cage with mirrors, so that the poor little creature will finish up by singing itself to death! And when the bird dies, our Dorabella will also die."

Lady Honoria was weeping by this time, and so was Dorabella herself. Sir Dauntless rose to his feet and took Dorabella's hand in his.

"Have no more fear, lady," he told her. "My heart is pure, and so I do not fear the wickedness of Arriman. I will be your champion against him."

Dorabella wiped the tears from her sapphire blue eyes and raised her moongold head to smile at Sir Dauntless. Her smile gave all the thanks she could not speak, but the Lady Honoria and Sir Veritas also thanked him on her behalf. Then all three followed behind as he strode out to mount Midnight again.

Dorabella knew, by this time, that she had fallen quite in love with this brave and handsome knight. But what if he should be killed by the demon magic of Arriman? True love would protect him, she thought; and told herself:

"I must give him something that belongs to me,

to be a shield for him against the powers of Arriman."

Shyly, then, she handed up to Sir Dauntless her handkerchief of fine blue silk. He took it from her, gently kissed it; and in a ringing voice he said:

"Lady, I am the Knight of the Golden Plain; and I swear by this love token that I will set your voice free to fly back to you. And then, one day, I will ask you to marry me."

S ir Dauntless turned Midnight's head towards Rapid River, and urged the great horse to a gallop.

Thud, thud, went his hooves. *Thud, thud,* echoed the sound over the whole of the Golden Plain. And when Arriman the demon magician heard that sound, he knew that Sir Dauntless was on the way to give him battle.

"Beware!" Sir Dauntless shouted as he rode, and flourished his sword. "Beware The Knight of the Golden Plain!"

Midnight galloped all the harder at this shout. But Rapid River was some distance away, and so it was still quite a time before they reached it.

Wide and deep it lay before them, then. Black and sullen were its waters. Swiftly these waters flowed with the rapid current that had given the river its name. And there was no bridge over it.

Sir Dauntless looked at the Dark Forest on the other side of the river, and knew he had no choice except to swim Midnight across to it. But would even so strong a horse as Midnight be able to swim against that powerful current? Would he not be afraid when he felt it pulling against him?

Sir Dauntless patted Midnight's neck. "Do your best for me," he said softly; and urged Midnight towards the challenge of the swift, dark waters.

Bravely the faithful creature answered to the challenge. One plunge took him right out into the fiercest part of the current. And with head held high then, he swam against it.

The shock of that plunge knocked the breath from Sir Dauntless; yet still he managed to stay upright in the saddle. And still Midnight was managing to swim against the force of water that battered at them both.

Powerfully he kicked out against it. Tightly Sir Dauntless clung to his reins. Rapid River roared and thundered all around them. Rapid River had them in its grip; a drowning grip. Yet still the faithful Midnight was struggling to free them both. And still, somehow, the further bank seemed to be drawing nearer.

With one last mighty effort, Midnight reached the further bank. He scrambled up the bank. And with a great cheer and a cry of "Brave fellow! Oh, brave fellow, Midnight!" Sir Dauntless knew they were safe at last.

But other dangers lay just ahead, of course; the dangers of the Dark Forest. And they would be the most terrible ones of all.

Sir Dauntless eyed the great dark mass of trees that loomed up only two minutes' ride away. And as soon as he and Midnight had got their breath back, he rode off towards it.

The trees of the Dark Forest were big, and old, and thick, and ugly. They were twisted into forms that had crumpled the bark of their trunks into the shape of strange and threatening faces. Their roots poked above the ground like a tangle of snakes writhing. They grew so close together, also, that their branches quite blotted out the light from the sky above. And down below, where the roots writhed, the spaces between the trees were filled with a dense growth of thorny bushes.

"There is no path," Sir Dauntless said when he saw all this; "and so, Midnight, I cannot ride you further."

He slid from the saddle and took a firm grip of his sword.

"Wait here for me," he added, and strode on alone into the Dark Forest.

The Dark Forest was soundless as well as dark. No birds sang in the trees. No small creatures scurried on soft feet through the bushes. It was cold there too, shut off from all the sunlight, but Sir Dauntless was soon warm with clearing a path for himself.

Slash, slash, he swung his sword at the dense undergrowth; and with every stroke of the sharp blade there were more of its thorny stems laid low. *Slash, slash;* and with every stroke he was deeper into the Forest. But how far did it stretch?

Sir Dauntless paused to look around him. Still nothing but trees; great, misshapen old trees like a regiment of ancient and crippled giants massed on every side of him. And where, among them, was the little golden singingbird held captive?

At the center of the Dark Forest, Sir Veritas had said. But, Sir Dauntless wondered, how was it possible to know if this slashing path really would lead to the center?

"I will hear the bird sing!" he thought suddenly. "And then I will know the way to the center!"

No sooner had this thought sprung to his mind than he heard a sound breaking the cold and deadly silence of the Dark Forest. The sound came from close at hand, and it was only a single note of music. But the note was so clear, and so piercingly

sweet, that Sir Dauntless knew instantly it could have been made by no other than the singingbird.

With a cry of joy, he turned towards the sound. Another note followed on from it, and then another. Then came a little trill of notes. The trill was followed finally by such a burst of song that the whole of the Dark Forest seemed to have become one vast cage of nightingales. And all the

time this sound was growing, Sir Dauntless was
hacking and slashing a way towards it.

The thorny bushes ripped at his hands and face.
His scarlet jerkin was torn too; but still he fought
on until, breathless but triumphant at last, he
reached the center of the Dark Forest.

There was a small clearing among the trees, he
saw then.

One single tree stood at the center of this clearing; a young and slender tree. Hanging from a branch of the young tree was a little cage that glittered brightly, both inside and out. The outside glitter came from its bars of silver. The inside glitter was from the mirrors that lined the bottom half of the bars. And the singing came from a tiny golden bird that dashed itself in despair against the silver bars, even while it sang.

Sir Dauntless let out a shout of rage at this pitiful sight; then he rushed forward and pulled open the door of the cage.

Swift as a ray of sun glancing, the little bird sped forth. Bright as a ray of sun gleaming, it soared up to disappear beyond the treetops. And the moment it was free of the Dark Forest was the moment when Dorabella cried:

"Oh!" Mouth and eyes round with astonishment, she repeated, "Oh!" And then, in a burst of delight she cried to Sir Veritas and Lady Honoria, "I can speak again. Oh, oh, oh, did you hear me? I can speak again!"

But in that same moment also, Sir Dauntless found himself at last facing the challenge of Arriman.

rriman appeared in the clearing in the Dark Forest like smoke rising out of the ground. The smoke billowed out into a cloud. The cloud shifted and changed in outline till it had formed the figure of a man. The man shape made of smoke grew solid and became Arriman in his long demon robes of slime green and rusty black and rotting purple.

Sir Dauntless felt even his brave heart grow faint before this sight. He shrank back from Arriman, and Arriman grinned a dreadful grin before he snarled accusingly:

"You took my golden bird from me!"

"The bird was Dorabella's voice," Sir Dauntless retorted; "and so I set it free to fly back to her."

"I will punish you for that," Arriman hissed.

He shot out his hands; long hands with a nail like a blood-red talon at every fingertip. He pointed the talons at Sir Dauntless, and howled one single and terrible word of magic.

Jets of flame spurted from the blood-red talons and roared straight at the face of Sir Dauntless. But

faster than the flames could travel, he shielded his face with Dorabella's handkerchief of fine blue silk; and the flames that touched it withered and died before the power of true love that was in it.

"And now it is my turn!" Sir Dauntless cried. "But I need no magic words, demon. I need only this!"

He swung his sword up and dealt Arriman a blow that split him clean in two, from the crown of his head downwards. But the two halves of Arriman only laughed two separate laughs, and then came together again as though nothing had happened.

"You foolish knight!" Arriman taunted. "There is nothing can conquer me; nothing in this world. And so you certainly cannot do it with your sword. Therefore, Sir Dauntless, Knight of the Golden Plain, prepare to breathe your last, here beneath the trees of the Dark Forest—every one of which I shall now command to fall down and crush and kill you!"

Arriman raised both arms high to the giant trees all around them both. He looked upwards, his green face glowing with a weird, unearthly light. And, as if he had already spoken his magic words of command, all the trees creaked and groaned and bent their great, heavy branches towards him.

"I am about to die!" thought Sir Dauntless. And could see no way to avoid this fact.

As every knight should do, then, when he sees death approaching, he knelt to say his prayers. He held his sword up before him as he knelt, the tip of it pointing downwards and the shape of the hilt between his clasped hands making the sign of the Holy Cross.

"Let this Holy Cross be the last thing my eyes look on before I die," Sir Dauntless prayed. And closed his eyes, waiting for the trees to fall on him.

Much to the astonishment and relief of Sir Dauntless, however, the trees did not fall. The moment he had spoken this last prayer, in fact, they ceased their creaking and groaning; and the sound he heard instead was a dreadful scream from Arriman.

Cautiously he looked up, and saw the demon magician staggering back from the holy sign made by the sword hilt. Sir Dauntless sprang to his feet.

"So!" he cried triumphantly. "There is nothing in this world can conquer you, you said. But you forgot one thing, did you not? You forgot the power of the Cross that is of this world and yet is of Heaven too. And by this Cross I hold now, Arriman, you *are* conquered!"

The demon magician's face turned from green to purple, and then to black. He fell to the ground, clutching at his throat and making horrid, choking noises. Sir Dauntless towered over him, holding the Cross high; and before his very eyes, a further change came over Arriman.

He shrank in size till he was only half as big as he had been before. His long robes became just like a bundle of rags about him. His face and head withered until they looked just like a burst and wrinkled leather ball. His limbs withered too, until they were just like sticks poking out from the rags that had been his robes.

Arriman had changed, in fact, to nothing more than an old scarecrow. And like a scarecrow now he lay, lifeless, and no longer able to harm anyone. Sir Dauntless turned to leave him, and immediately had a further surprise.

The Dark Forest had also changed. The trees there were still big and old, certainly; but now they were all spaced so much further apart from one another that he could see blue sky between their branches.

There was nothing threatening now, either, in the faces that had been shaped from the crumpled bark of their trunks. These faces, in fact, now had a sort of grandfatherly look about them instead.

And the bushes, the thorny bushes that had
been so closely crowded before, were now also
spaced much further apart. Besides which, the
bushes had all come suddenly into bloom!

They were covered with roses—clusters of small
white roses that made it seem as if they had been
scattered with a surprise shower of scented summer snow.

With great joy in his heart at all this, Sir Daunt-

less ran from the Dark Forest which was dark no
more. And saw, as he ran, some of the little
scurrying creatures that had come back to live in
it; heard, as he ran, the birds that had returned to
sing in the trees.

At the edge of the Forest, Sir Dauntless found
Midnight obediently waiting for him; and swing-
ing himself into the saddle, he rode the short
distance back to Rapid River.

He was not looking forward to crossing this again; but once he reached it, he found yet another surprise waiting for him.

Rapid River had also shrunk! It was as wide as it had been before—or nearly so, at least; but instead of being deep with a swift current running through it, its waters were now shallow and rippling pleasantly over a clean pebbly bed.

Sir Dauntless rode Midnight cheerfully through the shallow waters, and prepared to journey back to Crag Castle. But suddenly then, a thought struck him.

Crag Castle, he had remembered, was quite a distance away. If he rode back to it now, he would certainly be late home for tea. And most certainly then, also, his lady mother would be extremely angry with him.

Sir Dauntless sat wondering what he should do.

He had no wish to upset his lady mother, who had very strict rules about mealtimes. Yet he did not like the thought, either, of disappointing Dorabella.

On the other hand, he argued to himself, the golden singingbird had flown free, which meant that Dorabella would now be happy in having her voice back. And now also, Arriman was just an old scarecrow who could not possibly do her any more harm.

One more thing Sir Dauntless remembered then. On Saturdays there was always chocolate cherry cake for tea; and next to strawberries and cream, that was the thing he liked best.

The thought of Dorabella began to fade from the mind of Sir Dauntless. He could always see her another day, he decided; and turned Midnight's head homewards.

Back across the Golden Plain he rode, a brave and gallant figure in scarlet on his great black horse—Sir Dauntless, the scourge of witches, the slayer of dragons, the conqueror of the demon magician Arriman.

Fast, he rode. A knight grows hungry doing good deeds, and if he was late for tea he might miss his share of the chocolate cherry cake.

Further and further grew the distance between Sir Dauntless and Crag Castle. And the further he drew from it, the more like a rock it seemed to become. Dimmer and dimmer in his mind grew the picture of the beautiful Dorabella; and the dimmer this picture became, the quieter it grew in the tower room where she and the Lady Honoria and Sir Veritas had been rejoicing over the return of her voice.

Lady Honoria took up her sewing again. Sir Veritas stood looking from the window. Dorabella sat before the mirror combing her hair. She watched the comb rippling through the long moongold tresses, and spoke at last in a wistful voice.

"I wonder why Sir Dauntless has not come back yet."

"Probably," said Lady Honoria, "because he has gone home for tea. It *is* nearly teatime, after all."

"But he will come back another day," Sir Veritas added. "I promise you that, Dorabella."

Dorabella stared at herself in the mirror and saw her own sapphire blue eyes become full of longing for this promise to be a true one.

"How can you be sure of that?" she asked.

"Because, my darling," Sir Veritas told her, "the Golden Plain is not a place; it is a *time*. It is the time of long, golden summer days when you are young; the carefree days when you can spin yourself a daydream of any kind of adventure you wish to have. And Sir Dauntless *is* young, so that he is sure to seek many more adventures yet."

"But will he remember me?" Dorabella asked wistfully. "Will he?"

"Of course," Sir Veritas told her; "because the knight who dreams of rescuing a beautiful maiden in distress will ever afterwards keep the thought of her in his heart. That is how it always has been, Dorabella. And that is how it always will be."

Dorabella raised her comb again, slowly, and held it poised while she listened to Sir Veritas adding:

"And so you must wait, Dorabella, for the brave

Sir Dauntless. Wait until he does come back someday. Someday… Someday…"

The voice of Sir Veritas had been getting slower
and slower, and now it had faded into nothing. As
it faded, the hand of Lady Honoria faltered in its
sewing. Halfway through a stitch her needle came
to a stop. Dorabella's hand with the comb poised
above her moongold hair became very still. Sir

Veritas, too, became very still, until finally there was no movement at all, and no sound either, in the tower room. And in the rest of the castle, it was the same.

The soldiers on the battlements, the children who had played with the bright-colored ball, the cooks and other servants in the kitchen—all of them stopped what they were doing; and all of them, too, became as still and silent as statues of themselves.

There was no stirring of any kind of life at all in Crag Castle, in fact—except for one thing.

Just as Sir Dauntless arrived home and prepared to dismount from Midnight, his thoughts went tenderly back to Dorabella. And it was just then, also, that a sound floated down from the tower room—a little whispering echo of a sound that called faintly in the sweet tones of Dorabella's voice:

Come back...come back...come back...

Sir Dauntless, of course, could not possibly have heard so faint and faraway a cry. Yet still he went in to tea vowing to himself that he would go back very soon to see Dorabella and show her that he was a loyal knight, as well as a brave one.

Next Saturday, in all probability, he decided. Early next Saturday he would ride to Crag Castle, kneel at Dorabella's feet, and offer her all his fame and fortune.

And after that? After that, thought Sir Dauntless, he would spend the whole of the rest of the day galloping abroad on Midnight, once more doing good deeds and having great adventures.

No danger would be too great for him to face then. All evildoers would run in terror from him. And so once more also, he would prove himself to be indeed that bravest of all knights, Sir Dauntless; that most noble of all knights—

The Knight of the Golden Plain.